Across The Plain Where Five Remain

Michael V Punch

Illustrated by:
Chathura Jeewantha

ISBN: 0692069550
ISBN-13: 978-0692069554 (Da Formula Ent Presents)

Dedication

To my son Mitchell Punch
and to all young scholars around the world.

I'm reaching out to you all with a full heart in request
that you seek, understand your talent and
use it to it's fullest potential. There's
no cutting corners with excellence, you were born great.

The smile of a child is proof that there's
a better tomorrow so your state of being is well cherished.

I was told we stand on
the shoulders of our ancestors not to
weaken their knees, but to assist and
reach heights to find a better position for the crown.

I am the legacy, you are the legacy,
together "we are forever."

Hot and dry from the Zimbabwe sun, there's still a
lot to do that's fun. Elley was an elephant and the
last girl to be born in her herd of 23. She had
an older brother who hated to play. He was grumpy,
so Elley called him Gary Gray.

During the time of the year when it's very hot, and the cool breezes and the rain stop, Elley's herd headed east because that's where the water was. All the parents called for their kids.

"Elley, Elley!" Elley's mom called, but Elley was busy chasing an iguana. She was so busy that she ran away from everybody, and before she knew it, the whole herd was gone.

"Where did they go?" asked Elley.
"Mom, Dad!" she yelled, but there was
no answer. She got scared and ran, but she stopped
because she heard noises coming from the bushes.

"Who is that?" she said, trembling.
It was a hyena! She ran away, looking back to
see if the hyena was still behind her. The hyena ran ferociously
with her tongue hanging out.
Elley screamed for help. "Helppppp!!! Anybody!
Mom, Dad, Gary, somebody, please!"

But something happened that changed everything.
A jaguar named Jerald, whom everyone had feared and heard
stories about, showed up unexpectedly. Elley stopped
right in her tracks, causing her to fall and roll. She was rolling
so fast she rolled right over Jerald the jaguar and
squashed him. The hyena laughed and laughed until her
stomach hurt. The jaguar got upset and
decided to chase them both.

"Run," said the hyena to Elley. "Run! I think he's catching up. Keep on going. Don't look back before we run outta time."

Jerald got hurt when he got squished. He gave up the chase and stared after them. Elley and the hyena stopped running when they saw that he was no longer following them.

"Hey," Elley said to the hyena. "Are you running from him, too?"
Laughing, the hyena said, "Duh! Didn't you catch a clue?"
"What's so funny?" asked Elley.
"I'm a hyena. I laugh at everything; I can't help it."
"Why were you chasing me?" asked Elley.
"I was hungry," said the hyena.
"Can't you see I really wanted something to eat?"
"I'm not a snack, so you can stop it now with that," Elley told her.
The hyena laughed. "Sorry,
I can't help it. But you seem like a nice elephant."

Proudly, Elley said, "I am the last girl of 23,
and no one is as cool as me."
The hyena continued to laugh. "What's your name?"
"Elley. What's yours?"
"I'm Ena."

"Now that we're cool," Elley said, "don't try to eat me again."
Ena laughed, then mumbled under her breath,
"Now I'm hungry and thirsty."
Elley said, "Me, too. My herd went to find water."
"I know where water is," said Ena. "It's this way. Follow me!"

While walking in the hot sun, they regretted
ever having deciding to run. Elley and Ena were
really thirsty, and there was no water in sight.

They heard a rattle. They tried to
pretend they hadn't, but there it was again.
"What is that?" they both said to
each other, trying to look through the clutter.

They saw a tiny rattlesnake that said, "It's little ole me."
He was a baby rattlesnake named Rattles, and all the
time he liked to babble.
"I'm lost," said Rattles. "Where are you guys going?"

Elley said, "We're heading east to find something to drink."
Rattles said, "Hmmm, let me think. It's this way!
Whenever my mom went for food she took this
route, and I'm certain we'll find it without a doubt."

Elley said, "You lost your family, too?"
Rattles said, "Yes."
Ena did as well.
Rattles said, "Let's head to the forest,
far from where the lions dwell."

"So, wait," Elley said, "we all lost our parents?
This is strange. Maybe somehow it's all a game."
Ena said, "No, I was too busy playing around."
"So was I," Elley admitted.
Rattles stopped and started to cry. "Why, why, why?"

They finally reached the forest. Upon walking in, what did they
see? A monkey in a banana tree. He threw a banana,
and it hit Elley right in the face. SPLAT!!!

Ena laughed, but Rattles was scared.
Elley said, "Silly monkey. What was that for?"
The monkey said, "Hmmm, I've never seen you guys before.
What brings you here to the north?"

"North!" they all cried at the same time.
"I thought we were heading east!"
"By the way, my name is Pico. My parents named me that because
I like to pick fruits. What are your names?"
"I'm Elley the elephant," said Elley.
"I'm Ena the hyena," said Ena.
"I'm Rattles the rattlesnake," said Rattles.

"And I'm Jerald, the mean hungry jaguar!" Jerald shouted,
jumping out of the bushes and showing his teeth.

Pico quickly climbed up the tree and threw a
banana in Jerald's eyes. "HURRY!" Elley cried.
"Let's go, guys, while he can't see!"

Ena, Pico, and Rattles all agreed. While running through the forest as fast they could, they all started to become familiar with this strange land. Pico said, "Hey, I see water!"

Ena, Elley, and Rattles were excited, but they were also scared because they knew Jerald the jaguar was hiding somewhere. By then, they were all hot and weak.

Elley said, "My throat's so dry I can hardly speak.

Wait a minute!!! Is that my mom and dad?"
Ena said with joy, "Wait, I think I see my mom, too!"
Rattles and Pico said, "Yes, it's true! Our parents are here, too."

Jerald the jaguar jumped right in front of them. "Boom!"
he said. "This time you're all Gonna pay!"
And you wouldn't believe who saved the day—Elley's grumpy
older brother, Gary Gray.
"Yaaay!" they all screamed.
He told Jerald, "You're not as tough as you seem."

Another jaguar arrived and said, "Jerald, where were you? I was looking all over for you." Jerald said, with his head down, "Sorry, Mom. I was playing with my new friends." The mother jaguar looked at Elley, Ena, Pico, and Rattles and said, "Is this true?"

Everyone paused. Then Elley said, "Yep, he's part of our crew." The mother jaguar looked at Jerald and said, "Play nice, ok?" Jerald said, "Yes, ma'am. But this time, please don't go far away." They all laughed. Jerald said, "Thanks for not telling on me, you guys. It's just I was just so hungry and thirsty. I promise I won't do it again." Rattles said, "Does that makes us all friends?" Ena laughed, while Elley said, "I think we're all gonna be the best of friends and grow old together."

They all looked at all the water.
"What an adventure," said Elley. "Now it's time to fill our bellies."
They all ran over to the water to drink, laugh, and play.
They reunited with their families and hung around for hours.

"We couldn't of asked for anything more," said Elley.
But one thing was for sure: from here on out, things would
never be the same. "My name is Elley and this is my story,
'Across the Plain Where Five Remain.'"

Elephants are the world's largest land-living mammal.
The word "elephant" comes from the Greek
word "elephas" which means "ivory".
There are two types of elephant, the African elephant and the
Asian elephant. But sometimes the African Elephant is split
into two species, the African Forest Elephant
and the African Bush Elephant.

Hyenas use various sounds, postures and signals
to communicate with each other.
Spotted hyenas "laugh" as a form of communication to
relay excitement or frustration. This vocalization
can often be heard during a hunt.

The jaguar has the strongest bite force of any cat and the strongest bite of any mammal. With that bite force, jaguars will crunch down on bones and eat them. In fact, in the zoo, bones are part of a jaguars' regular diet.

Rattlesnakes get their name from special structures on the tip of their tail. Their "rattle" is made of rings of keratin (the same material our fingernails are made of). When vibrated, the rattle creates a hissing sound that warns off potential predators. It is an extremely effective and highly evolved predator-avoidance system.

Monkeys are furry animals with long, fur-covered
tails and hands with thumbs.
There are more than 260 different species of monkeys in the world.
Monkeys are often divided into old world monkeys and new world
monkeys, depending on where they live in the world.
The New World monkeys live in the Americas, while Old World monkeys
live in Asia and Africa.